I0757266

THE
INVENTOR'S
Journal
Workshops
from 2020

Dedicated to my Big Sister
ANNIE

Her creative talent inspires mine.

Other books by LJ Kidd ~ Dyslexic writer

www.fartintothedarkness.com

LJ is Available for creative workshops for all ages.

The Inventor's Journal

Footprints for the future

Written and illustrated by

LJ Kidd

The Original
Popsicle

THE
CLAW

SCHOOL
smile ü

Chapter One

The Inventors Journal

"Pigs breath," Dickson yelled at the top of his voice standing as tall as a short boy could. Punching his chest like King Kong gone wrong, Dickson has currently lost interest in my Inventors Journal class, and I thought all this time he was having a blast.

Hello. My name is Miss Annie and I'm the visiting teacher in this class today. An inventors journal we are making, footprints for the future is what I say, because our ideas could lead the way.

There is a history of young inventors that I've shared with this class, I would love them to see that it's possible to be.

Up till now, all the kids have been working well. Creating their covers, pasting their pages and some kids have already got ideas of inventions they could make. Except Dickson, he seems to think this class is a big mistake.

He finds it hard to sit and no sooner is his bum on the seat and he's back on his feet.

"Pigs breath, pigs breath, pigs breath," Dickson yelled again, over and over, words all sounding the same. Clumsily he climbed to the top of his desk and started to kick the pages of his journal into the air, they went flying everywhere.

Dickson's Inventor's Journal scattered and I was shattered.

Lilico stood quietly to her feet, "Miss Annie,"
she said with a certain Japanese charm.
"Please tell Dickson to stop and sit down, he's
acting like a silly, class clown." Her sweet Japanese
eyes were replaced with a long, strong, Aussie glare,
but Dickson, he didn't care.

Lilico didn't want the class to end
and didn't want to be distracted, but
Dickson instead of sewing his journal
together like the other kids, he made
his pages fly, don't ask me why?

"Pigs breath," Dickson yelled once more, "I'm a pig hunter," he barked, " I work with pigs not with books," he yelled as the last pages landed flat on the classroom floor.

I whispered "pigs breath" myself, then getting the attention of the class, I said… "Pigs breath, pigs breath, pigs breath." Directing with my hand for the class to join in, I sung the words loud, "Pigs breath, pigs breath, pigs breath."

Some kids sung high, Jackson sang perfectly low and played his piano like he was in a show. The Irish twins Donna and Daniel did an Irish spin, Lilico sung her lungs proud and her sister Miico made her pigs breath, very loud.
I continued to direct with my hand as if I was on an orchestra stand.

"Pigs breath, pigs breath, pigs breath," I sung again. Dickson didn't know what to do but he found it funny too.

Suddenly high pitched screams filled the room,
"What now?" I thought.

Dickson had dropped his pants just enough for
a large fart to go, PUFF.

All the Inventors Journals became fans for farts
as the disgusting perfume filled the class. "Farting
outside please," I spoke briskly to Dickson.

"We are all doomed," called Jackson pinching his
nose and pretending to die. "Yes, farting outside,"

Lilico repeated with her fan in hand directing
the air elsewhere.

"Pigs breath, smelly bum," Daniel said,
but a number of kids fingers pointed his way,
reminding him of his own farting days.

The class laughed but I laughed even more
because something I haven't as yet said, today was
school dress up day and all the kids were dressed
in very funny ways.

I didn't know it was dress up today, the
teachers forgot to say. But next week when I do
my last class, I will be the surprise because I will
dress up for their eyes.

Chapter Two

Dress Up Day

There were soldiers and dancers, fire twirling sticks, animals, fishing rods and all kinds of cool, costume tricks. Dickson gave off another fart and ran across the room to the door of his escape, only to be greeted by his biggest mistake.

The Headmaster. Mrs Shellshock.

She stood at the door wanting to know more. "Back to class please," she spoke stretching her cat like arm to catch Dickson by his piggy ear.

Mrs Shellshock was dressed as a BABY and
her dummy sucking was hysterically CRAZY.
She wore flamboyant, flamingo, pyjamas, nappy
pins frequently placed, and held a teddy right up
to her face. I don't know why but that Teddy
caught my eye.

"Please pay attention to the last of the class,"
Mrs Shellshock said but pretended it was her
Teddy speaking instead. That Teddy has spy eyes
leaving me curious to say, he's much more than
just part of the dress up day.

Lilico for dress up was proud in her traditional
Japanese gown. Jackson was dressed in a suit and
an orange tie. A piano strapped to his chest,
Elton John would think he was the best.

Daniel and Donna the Irish twins, well they
were all dressed in green, with green hair and
green tongues, Daniel even spoke to all the kids
about his green… bum.

"I'm a pig hunter," as we know, this is Dickson
and he was dressed to show. Camouflaged clothes
held up with a belt, rumbling socks collected by
big boots, and a large display of weapons in a
plastic ways. His broad hat spoke with feathers of
the past and a big tooth around his neck showed
me he had smelt the breath of a pigs head.

Whispers in my ear told me Dickson dresses
like this every day, but to me he looked ok.

I smiled ~ thinking of next week's class and how
to dress up as a laugh. I won't let the kids know,
not even Mrs Shellshock, not a clue I would show.

Chapter Three

Some Inventors Stories

"Before you all go today, I would like to ask about some of the inventions we have spoken about in class." I sounded my bell that tickled the air to keep everyone there.

"Who remembers Frank Epperson and what did he invent," I asked the class, bell high ready to ring. Lilico's hand was first, she has been listening to my every word. I rang the bell for her to speak, she stood to her feet and adjusting her Japanese gown, she spoke clear and sound.

"He invented the ice block Miss Annie," she said with a polite bow of her Japanese head.

"He was only eleven when he invented that,"
I spoke making sure they understood that their
age wasn't important at this stage.

"One more question then you can go," quickly
speaking to hold the class and ringing my bell fast.
Mrs Shellshock still sucking her dummy, turned
Teddy's ear so he could hear.

"What did George Nissen invent and what did
he write in his journal that night?"

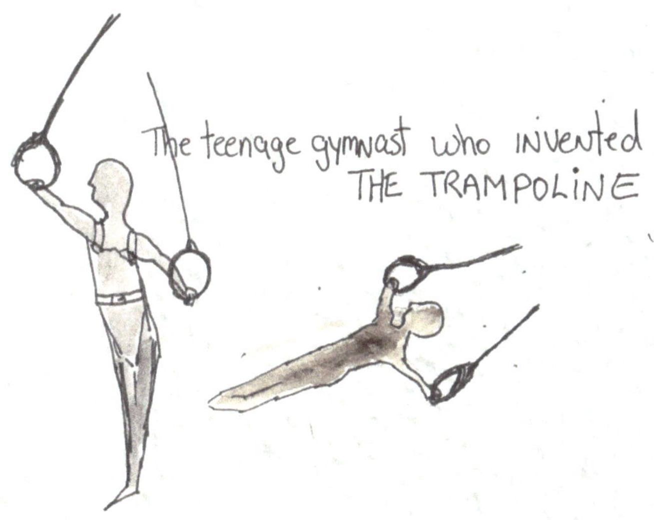

Daniel this time was fast, "a trampoline," he said quickly bouncing around in all his green. "He did the trapeze Miss Annie, and when he fell into the net he thought up a trampoline instead."

Daniel was correct. Again I rang my bell but that wasn't' the only noise in the room, Mrs Shellshock sucking her dummy sounded like a noisy vacuum.

"He was sixteen," Donna called out and started to also bounce about. The green Irish twins did a trampoline spin.

Mrs Shellshock took her dummy out & waiting for the class, "No matter what age, the colour of your skin, where you were born or your past. If you have a good invention write it down, we will help you get it made, and then you can say, what a great day." Mrs Shellshock's dummy went straight back into her mouth.

"Ink your ideas onto the page and they just might happen one day," I said while lifting my own journal to show a page that has my invention idea displayed. The journals were placed on my desk, all the kids have done their best, even Dickson had an invention on his page I looked forward to reading it later that day.

"Teddy would like to go home with you Miss Annie," Mrs Shellshock said placing Teddy on the pile of journals. "He has an old fashion touch from the past, you might enjoy it and laugh."

What could a Bear do if it just has stuffing and glue? But I accepted the gift and ringing my bell this class has finished very well.

Mrs Shellshock went back to being a baby for the last of the day and waved for the kids to go on their way. "Pigs breath," Dickson yelled once more as he ran for the door.

"Duck Power," Mrs Shellshock yelled back. Holding her duck necklace high and allowing it to move side to side, "Flap your beaks and have your say, one of you could become an inventor one day."

"Goodbye Miss Annie," I heard a number of times like a beautiful rhyme. "I will see you again soon," I said with a smile, remembering next week will be my dress up surprise treat.

Chapter Four

Teddy

Not the Real Toy

The week flew by like birds in the sky and
today was the last class and I finally get to
have my own dress up blast.

But a strange happening overnight
at my place has left me curious to
say, Teddy isn't just stuffing and
glue, I'm sure he has that old
fashion magic too. Each night in
my house Journals have been on the
move but last night he has scattered
them all over my floor, one was
even at my front door.

Teddy was missing, and so was
Lilico and Dickson's journals.
What would I say in class today?
A Coffee fix for me is needed, so
on my way to Neo & Lucy's café.

No sooner did I arrive at the café and I heard Dickson's name spoken into the air, it looked like his Mum and she had the hand of her younger son. "Dickson," she called again. "Come on quickly, you will be late for school." But I couldn't see Dickson anywhere at all.

Suddenly, like a wild pig himself, from under the table crawled Dickson on all fours. He had been hiding and had the Bear, even Lilico was hiding under there. Teddy's spy eyes were alive.

"Could you please take these to class?" Lilico
and Dickson asked as they place their journals
and the bear in my hands. I was in a little daze
and their journals had a light glowing haze.

"Good morning Miss Annie," Teddy said in
a whispered voice. Leaping back in a fright my
coffee flew, he's more than stuffing and glue?
Did he really speak?

"Miss Annie it's ok," he said.

"But I need the dark Miss Annie to keep my.."
Abruptly, he stopped talking, "You need the
dark?" I asked. I quickly looked at the table, "yes"
I thought, its dark under there, do I dare?
The moment I had him under the table he's spy
eyes came back alive.

"I'm not just stuffing and glue," Teddy said,
I felt bad to say what I did, but I wasn't to know
in my head. Neo and Lucy with another coffee
for me came over, curious to see. "My stuffing
was wrong when I was first made, I wasn't a real
toy not like the old days. But I got fixed and
then I could do the old day tricks. I can come
alive at night when kids' eyes are closed and they
are snoring their nose.

I can hold a spell to make things well and most important I can say, I help children to see their way." Neo, Lucy and myself all moved in close to keep his space dark, we wanted to know all about Teddy's old fashioned spark.

"Is it a secret you coming alive?" I asked. "No secret," Teddy quickly said. "Things aren't made like the old days and kids don't believe and they watch too much TV." Both Lucy and I agreed.

He talked of how he got his spark and how he came to live with Mrs Shellshock but the most important, he spoke of the magic he has placed in the journals for our class today.

It was time for me to get dressed, remember, today is my dress up day and nobody knows, so best I get on the way. I don't want to be late on my very special last day.

Chapter Five

Queen of Hearts

"Miss Annie, Miss Annie," the children called
as they saw me arrive at their school. They were
delighted to have me back, wait till they see...

My car door shuts exposing my own dress up.
"STOP," I said loud and long
with a hand signal strong.

"Stop, in the name of the
Queen," I said. My nose
pointed high in the air as
the Queen of hearts would,
I'm from the very famous
Alice in Wonderland book.

"It's not dress up day," squawked Dickson.

"Off with his head," I quickly said pointing
my finger strong. Dickson laughed, then
snorted hard and of course let out another
puff of a smelly green fart.

"Off with all your heads,"
I spoke. pointing my finger
to make strong the joke.
My big red dress fell to the
ground with a tight corset
held all around. A large
starched collar around my
neck, hair high and lips
painted in a heart, I really
looked the part as a very
good Queen of Hearts.

The kids crashed my
space and wrapped their
arms around my waist,
with giggles in the air
and journals everywhere.

"It's time to start the class, and Dickson," looking him straight in the eye with my Queen of Heart lips tightly gripped. "NO more farts," I asked, he just laughed.

I walked like a Queen towards the class and everyone danced around and laughed. I placed Teddy in the hands of Lilico who knew the spell and was very excited to tell.

Mrs Shellshock was looking on pleasantly surprised at my dress up that caught her eye.

Chapter Six

THE JOURNAL SPELL

Dickson and Lilico's journals were glowing
even more by the time we all got through the
classroom door. Bums were on seats very fast
and I quickly told the class. "Teddy came home
with me and read all your journals, he was so
impressed that he left a spell for your journals
to show and tell."

We all watched as Dickson and Lilico
opened there journals wide, an exploding
rainbow was inside. Flashes of colour bounced
fast from each page, inspiring each journal
stage by stage.

All the journals came alive in a 3D way
with each invention hovering up off the page.
"It's impossible only if you believe it is,"
Lilico said watching her invention hover over
her head. "Teddy has done this," I said to the
kids and explained his power when it's dark.
They all watched and listened hard as each
invention sparked.

CHAPTER SEVEN

THE KIDS INVENTIONS

The class was alive with each idea hovering
high. I placed Teddy on my desk so he could
see. I had no way to make it dark so he could
have his spark, then I thought.

Placing a paper bag over his head with eyes
cut wide might be enough, it was worth a try.
His eyes blinked and feet moved, Teddy could
see, we were all very happy.

"Lilico, would you like to explain your
invention to the class?" I asked.
She was quick to her feet.
"I don't like to get
wet," was the first
thing she said. "My
invention is an umbrella
you don't have to hold.
Hover Dry I called it and
without a handle it follows you
around keeping you dry and sound.

The batteries can be charged by the sun and
it doesn't matter if its dark the Hover Dry will
still fly." Suddenly a small stream of rain fell
directly onto the Hover Dry. "See," Lilico said,
moving around and showing how it works...
"I'm not wet at all and it folds up very small."
The class clapped, I was amazed, what a clever
girl to think in this way.

"My invention is a steam punk drone," Dickson stood to his feet as the sparks of the rainbow glowed. His steam punk drone hovered over his head as he used his journal to direct and show all the instruments that he had on the go.

"My drone can do a number of things, find pigs for me to shoot, spy on the cows to make sure they are not getting out and, this lens here," Dickson turned the drone so we could all see, "you can time travel Miss Annie." The class continued to watch as Dickson explained each part but it was the death bullet that made the class laugh.

A speed gauge, temperature and movement
gauges and a sun powered water spray. A camera
to record and the time travel lens, a sleep bullet
and the claw, who would want more.

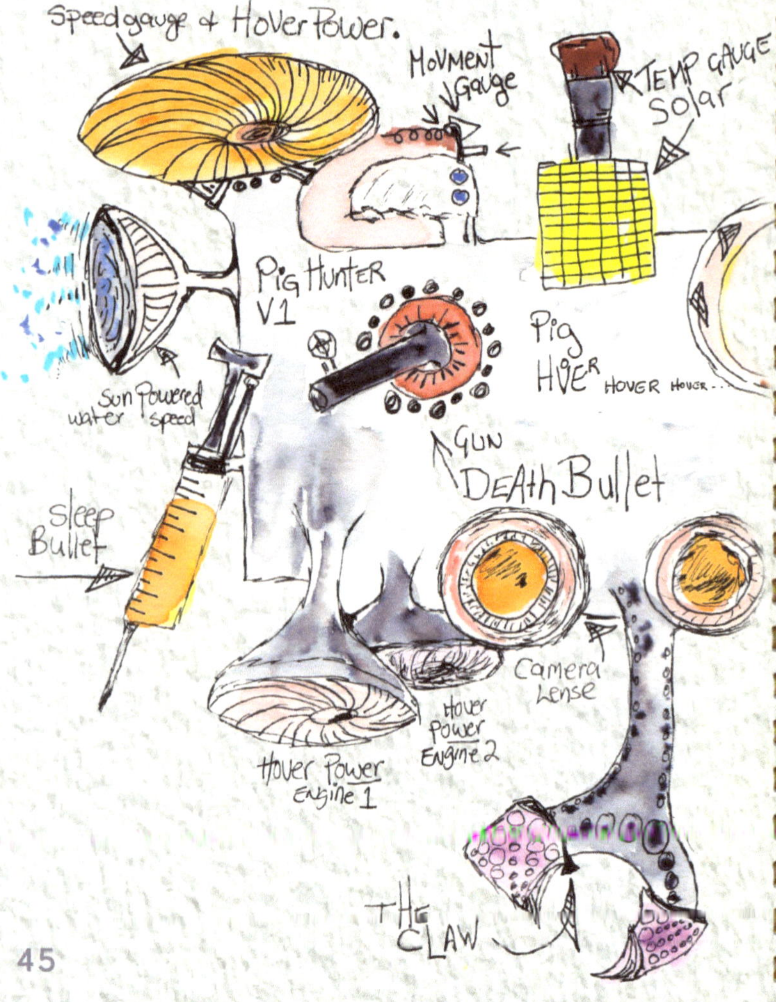

Slowly I started to clapped and the kids
felt the same, Dickson had won the day.
"Farmers are going to love your invention
Dickson," I said as he directed his drone
towards Teddy. "Not the death bullet,"
I quickly spoke as a silly classroom joke.

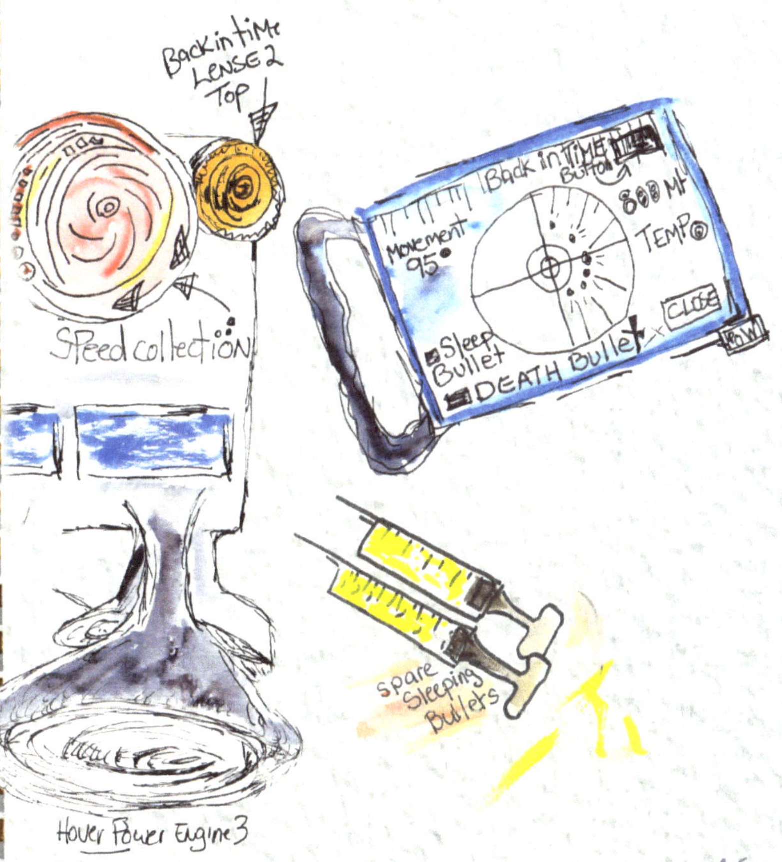

"I can fly Miss Annie," Jackson said with his spider man gloves flicking spider man web.

"There really is magic at the end of the rainbow," Donna was amazed watching her invention come alive in the rainbow haze.

Time passed in the class fast, everyone had their turn to explain they invention and their intention. Mrs Shellshock appeared at the door, "off with you head," I said pointing her way, she could see we have had a fantastic day.

The rain stopped. Dickson's drone flattened back onto the page. Lilico's Hover Dry folded away and all the rainbows had their last play.

No one really wanted to go, we were all so much enjoying the Inventors Journal show.

Duck Power

"A big clap of thanks for
Miss Annie," Mrs Shellshock said.
The room filled with sound as
I bowed and held my heart lips
ever so proud. "Duck Power,"
Mrs Shellshock called, all the class
stood tall. Mrs Shellshock held her
duck necklace and as it moved
up and down, "Duck Power," she said as all the
kids turned their heads the same way to say...

"Duck Power, Duck Power, quack quack
quack. What you have to say will make yourself
a good day." The class burst into laughs as
chatter spread across the room.

"I'm going to stay awake all night, I have lots of teddies on my bed." Donna said. "Remember to feed your journals each day, don't let one page get away," said Mrs Shellshock.

Gently I rang the bell but I was curious and intrigued. Out of the corner of my eye my own Journal glowed alive.

Teddy has left me some magic, how fantastic.
"Off with your head," I said once more to each
child leaving through the door. "These journals
are your footprints for the future," I spoke as
Mrs Shellshock chuckled at all my jokes.

I could see my glowing journal waiting for me...

www.ingramcontent.com/pod-product-compliance
Lightning Source LLC
Chambersburg PA
CBHW041732300726
48981CB00006B/322